Caribbean Heat
Baby Girl Book V

In the Beginning Book I
Moonlighting in Paris Book II
City by the Bay Book III
Bite the Big Apple Book IV
Caribbean Heat Book V
Return to the Bay Book VI
Prison of the Past Book VII
Baby Girl Box Set - a collection of books I-IV

Elle Klass

Caribbean Heat Baby Girl V

Caribbean Heat Baby Girl V

Author's Disclaimer

This book is entirely fictional. Any characters, places or events are purely figments of the author's imagination. No part of this publication may be reproduced, transmitted or redistributed either in its entirety or in part without the author's express written consent.

Caribbean Heat Baby Girl V

Other Young Adult Books by Elle Klass

St. Augustine Novellas
Bloodseeker Series
Book 1 The Vampires Next Door
Book 2 The Monster Upstairs
Book 3 The Ghost Within

hidden journals
Isandro

Zombie Girl
Book 1 Premonition
Book 2 Infection
Book 3 Retribution

The Box Set Recap
In the Beginning

In the Beginning. Twelve-year-old Cleo calls a shack in Brennan, California home. She lives there with her mother who is, at best, a part-time mom. Her mother disappears, leaving Cleo to fend for herself. With no other choice she jumps on board a train to the closest city.

In the city, she meets a gang of other child vagabonds, forms close friendships with them, and an especially close bond with Einstein their leader. Together the foursome begin a thieving spree in the name of survival. It is during a heist that two of the vagabonds are caught, leaving Cleo and Einstein on the run. They continue their act across the country, finally stopping when they have enough savings to start a life together.

They choose a southern city, settle, and start their quiet life. Einstein takes a job as a dishwasher and Cleo begins a lifelong love for cooking. Their love for each other deepens by the day. They make friends with their next door neighbors, James and his daughter, LulaBell. Cleo and LulaBell become friends and through LulaBell's studies, Cleo learns about Paris. As the heat from their past crimes resurfaces with copy-cat thefts, Cleo and Einstein decide to leave for Paris.

It is on their last night in the sleepy southern city that Cleo finds her life in turmoil. In a single moment, Einstein's life is violently taken. James offers to get Cleo a passport. She accepts his offer. Her new name: Justine Holmes.

Moonlighting in Paris

Moonlighting in Paris. Cleo takes on a new identity: Justine Holmes. She travels to Paris and meets Didier, a rich hotel owner. In no time, the two become very close. She gains information on her mother's disappearance and Einstein's death. Instead of answers, she finds mystery and people who want her dead. Didier, unaware of her shaded past but well aware of her strange behavior, hires a body guard, Sam, to keep an eye on her.

As her and Didier's relationship peaks, a new threat appears, a warning written in lipstick, while she's working in Aruba.

Justine doesn't know whether the threat is tied to her past or something in her present. Aware of the threat, unaware of her past, Sam and Didier keep her close. Didier proposes to her. Excited, she accepts. During their engagement party her new pursuer takes the threat up a notch, attempting her harm.

Justine takes matters into her own hands, stalking her stalker. Didier's lack of knowledge about her past, and her stubborn independence, lead to the accidental death of her stalker. The guilt hanging over her head and the mystery of her birth family lead her to make a heart wrenching decision. She leaves Didier the night before the wedding, sneaking out through her terrace window, and heads home to the U.S. to solve her own family mystery.

City by the Bay

In City by the Bay, Cleo takes the puzzle pieces involving her mysterious past and begins to link them together. She changes her identity to Shanna Nu and gains employment at the La Tige Detective

Agency. She learns Perdy kidnapped her to hide her from the Briggses. A wealthy, powerful family. To give Perdy's family closure, she visits them. Her mother, Leila, is still alive and welcomes Shanna into her home under the pretense that Shanna is a police officer. Shanna shares details of Perdy's death and leaves her with a number to call so she can claim and properly bury her daughter.

Shanna and La Tige become closer than coworkers. She begins to think of him as the father she never had. Likewise, he becomes attached to her. He drops clues involving her past but under no circumstances will she discuss it with him. After solving a big case, he gives her the key to his unsolved cases drawer. She digs through the files finding new information pertaining to Perdy's case along with an unrelated case involving a young woman, a baby, and a police officer. She takes the information and makes a decision to seek employment within the Briggs's infrastructure and go to New York.

Meanwhile, she has become best friends with Kacy, owner of the Happy Trails bar, and her roommate. In Happy Trails late one night she meets Fetch, a gorgeous hunk of man. Her and Fetch form a relationship of sorts. She is unable to trust in their relationship and leaves him, without warning, for New York. She says goodbye to Kacy and La Tige. Before boarding the plane she finds a note from La Tige in the phone he gave her. It is the address to a rent controlled apartment.

Bite the Big Apple

Shanna Nu travels to New York with a lead that is sure to bring her closer to her roots. She takes a job working for the Briggses. The company who employed Slug. Within a short time with the Briggses, William Briggs the third, Will, hires her as his executive secretary. Over the next several months her and Will become close and she learns he is her half-brother. La Tige gives her a lead, the number for a woman named Claudel Winters. Upon visiting her, she learns Claudel worked for her bio-mom, Celia Shariff. Cleo (Shanna) observes her bio-mom but is unable emotionally to make contact. Instead she flees New York after Will gives her a large sum of money, along with shares in the family business.

Cleo returns to the shack in California where she grew up and writes her auto-biography. She sends the manuscript to Einstein's parents, who own a publishing company. She met them while in New York, during a visit to his grave. They accept the manuscript and, with Cleo's assistance, set up a fund for runaway children. Cleo stays with his parents for a few days and learns Einstein's reason for running away. A mystery she puts on her list to solve.

While in New York, Fetch finds Cleo. His artwork got him a gracious offer from an art dealer. He assumes that with money and security Cleo will stay with him. After their romp, while he's sleeping, she sneaks out of his room, and vanishes from his life, ignoring his calls.

Cleo obtains her birth certificate and legally changes her name to Cleo Burke. Her emotional roller coaster far from over, she returns to Paris and glimpses Didier one last time. She can't face him, understanding finally that she loved him but wasn't *in* love. He was her knight in shining armor. The man who saved her from a lonely, homeless life. Not willing to hurt him again, she leaves and jet sets to parts unknown.

Paradise

Our backs laying on the sandy shore behind my St. Thomas house. The edge of the tide drifted over our feet and receded.

"Do you ever think you'll give her a chance?" asked Will, my half-brother. Born from the same father who, in my opinion, is a wicked, vile man. My dislike for him conflicted to the millionth degree with my sense that, in his own demented way, he loved me.

"I don't know. How could she let me go? She never searched, just took your - our - father's word for it. Since when does he tell the truth?" I glimpsed my bio-mom once, that's it, but couldn't bring myself to meet her. In my heart I knew I was tougher on her than my sperm donor father.

Will chuckled, his blond hair blowing in the breeze as he turned and lifted himself onto his elbows and turned towards me. "You're right. He doesn't tell the truth often. He is a tough, conniving man who's become more reserved since," he cleared his throat, "your last meeting." The last time I saw my sperm donor I intentionally poured red wine down his white, expensive dress shirt. It felt incredible!

I twisted onto my stomach and lifted myself onto my elbows and peered at Will through the long tufts of hair whipping across my face. "My entire life is like a daytime soap opera. Now it's my time... I've been many people: born as Camille, then Cleo, Justine and Shanna, and I won't mention mom-Perdy's name for me, now I'm legally Cleo Burke. I'm no longer that scared young girl with no roots, but a grown woman who wants nothing more than to put my past behind me and move forward with my life."

His eyes scanned the vast Caribbean. "I see. I've never seen such clear ocean water. This place makes me want to stay and say F-it. The business doesn't need me!" His voice mingled with the sound of the tide beating against the shore.

"Yup, why I chose it. It's breathtaking and the beaches are pure and crowded with palm trees. Dense, lush green plants cover the Earth. And the sunrise and sunsets are incredible." The sun lingered just above the ocean, sinking beneath the horizon. The colors of the sky reflected back from the ocean giving our eyes a breathtaking visual display.

We lay silent as the sun set over the ocean and the tide rolled in and out over our bodies. I bought a small beach house in St. Thomas. I had a home, a real home. It was small and modest but it was mine. It had three bedrooms and two baths separated by a vast expanse enclosing my kitchen, dining room and living room. Each bedroom accommodated a walk-in closet and my bath included a large tub with jets much like the one I enjoyed while living with Didier. And hot water - tons of hot water. A small bar stocked with fine wines and various rums separated the kitchen from the living room.

My decorations were light, as I liked the open airiness of my home. I framed pictures of myself and Einstein into a collage. A large screen door in the living room opened into a small patio and the beach just beyond, where Will and I lay now in the sand. I spent my time staring at the ocean and island skipping. Thanks to my brother's generous $250,000,000 and shares in the family business. I considered it back child support from my sperm donor.

Will visited whenever he got the chance. We adored each other. He's the only member of my bio-family I desired to spend time with and we shared it together acting like young children, catching up on the play time we missed. We golfed on the beach and when balls got pulled into the ocean the tide always brought them back. We learned to surf together, at first we did lots of falling off our boards together, but we've improved our skills.

Will stood and dusted the sand from his legs. "The sun is set - s'mores time." He strolled towards my patio, sand jumping from his feet with each step, and came back with wood.

While he tended to the fire I stood, not bothering to dust myself off, and padded inside to my pantry for Graham crackers, chocolate bars, marshmallows, and pokers.

My hands loaded with sweet treasures, I sat in the sand beside Will. "Whenever you tire of New York or divorce your bulldog wife," I looked at the scowl that washed across his face with the mention of his better half, "you always have a home here."

"Bulldog? Hmm... I think she's aged to look more like a Rottweiler." He guffawed, flashing brilliant, happy, green eyes my direction.

I met his laugh with a grin that took over the lower half of my face.

"So when is uh... Mr. La Tige coming in?" Will's visit was due to his eagerness to meet the fatherly figure in my life, La Tige. A man of few spoken words whose body language and heartfelt gestures say he loves me. I'm the daughter he never had. Will was staying long enough to meet him. He had to get back to New York and business before our evil demon-spawn sister, Patrice, found a loophole to take over the business and leave us out in the cold. Ha! I'd been there.

"Tomorrow. We're meeting him in San Juan and I've planned a small vacation excursion for him. He never relaxes like someone else I know." I shifted my eyes, giving him a sideways glance. "Someone with blond hair that has a blow over right now from the wind." He was always sensitive about his inherited male pattern baldness. The only trait he picked up from our father.

"You!" Is all he got out as I shoved my s'more into his gaping mouth. More of it landed on his lips and beneath his nose, giving him a s'mores mustache.

I fell backwards into the sand in laughter and found his s'more planted in my mouth. More s'mores made it into my mouth because it was open wide enough for a jet engine to fit! Pain from laughter shot though my abs as though I did a thousand crunches with weights tied to my chest. He leaned over and offered me a hand covered in s'more that he'd wiped from his face.

"Eww... You gave me cooties!" I leaned over to wipe the mess on his chest but he was too quick and slid backwards out of my reach.

"Yeah, it's time!" I voiced with seriousness and rose to my feet, sauntering inside the house. After washing my hands, I made two mudslides loaded with spiced rum. Rum was the way of the islands and I grew to love it.

I took my spot beside him on the beach, the vast Caribbean spread out before us, the tide humming as it rolled in and out. I handed him his drink and rested my head on his shoulder. Where we sat in silence admiring the visual display before us.

Black Widow

La Tige stepped off the plane in San Juan, as always, looking out of place in paradise. In the past I've tricked him into small cruises within the islands and we've dined on native Caribbean foods. It's not often I see him but he is my surrogate father and I love him as much as Will. Last visit I teased him about his attire. The Caribbean was a place of comfort and warm weather. His usual disheveled suit made him stand out. He took my advice this time and wore a polo shirt, shorts and flip flops, but his uptight gruffness still showed.

People in Puerto Rico worked on their own time clock and were always friendly. They didn't seem to understand the hustle and bustle of the states. I admired that about island life because, even though on U.S. soil, one would never know. It was like a foreign country all its own. I planned on keeping him in PR (Puerto Rico) for a couple days before heading to St. Thomas. I always picked him up here, but we never stayed, always heading to VI (Virgin Islands) in a rush, but not this time. There was so much to do and I made a goal to show him the richness of the island and provide him an actual vacation. I booked reservations at one of the most renowned resorts in the San Juan area and booked a limo to transport us from the airport into another world, resort life in PR.

He held a single carry-on bag, he packed light as he never stayed long; he walked towards me and wrapped an arm around my back in a half hug. Affection was not a strong point for La Tige but underneath he was like a child's much loved stuffed toy.

Will looked him over pensively and La Tige returned the visual cues. "Over protective brother Will, meet surrogate over protective father."

"La Tige." He extended his hand towards Will.

"Will. Pleasure to finally meet you Mr. La Tige." Will accepted La Tige's hand in a friendly shake.

"Now that's over with, how was the trip?" I asked.

"Long,"

"So what is on our agenda?" La Tige asked with undertones of *I know you have something planned.*

I smiled. "You know me too well. We are catching a limo back to a resort and you are taking an actual vacation."

"Glad I cleared my calendar for a couple days. Every time I visit you it's never simple. You are not simple." He countered with inflections of intrigue.

William piped in, shaking his head in dismay, "Women are never simple."

La Tige chuckled and turned his large bulk towards Will. "Never."

"I am what I am and you," I shifted my eyes from Will to La Tige, "will always be you. I want you to share in this alluring world in which I live. Look around you, is there anything more breathtaking in all the world?"

"No, I don't think there is." They responded in unison then stared at each other...

The limo driver waited where Will and I left him, he opened the doors for us while he took La Tige's single bag of luggage and stowed it in the trunk.

For a world lacking mainland hustle and bustle, the roads stayed packed with cars, making any trip slow going. It gave Will and La Tige a chance to talk.

At dinner that night we ate a delicious authentic meal with tostones on the side - one of my favorites - and I ate them like one might eat potato chips. They are a simple recipe of mashed, fried plantains and are delightful. After dinner we relaxed on the beach with drinks. Fine French wine would always be my favorite but, like any place, PR had its version of fine alcohol- rum! The rum here isn't just rum, but a recipe they have made into an art. I grew to love a good Mojito; my choice of fine Caribbean drink. La Tige was much simpler and drank rum and cokes. Will settled on drinking the local beer, Medalla.

I was on cloud nine spending the evening with the two most important men in my life! A refreshing breeze blew from the ocean.

Will and La Tige got along like old friends sharing silly Cleo stories at my expense. After several drinks and light conversation, Will stood. "I have an early morning, good night, sis." I stood and gave him a hug and peck on the cheek. "Mr. La Tige, take care of her. She's a fragile one." I kicked his shin, causing him to scowl playfully.

"Night." La Tige, still sitting, extended his hand and pulled Will in for a quick half hug.

I returned to my seat and La Tige leaned towards me and with a gentle voice, not a usual attribute, he said, "Thank you for doing all this. I don't take vacations or slow long enough to enjoy life."

"You're welcome. You've done many things for me and I want to give you a little back. This place is like no other. It's easy to lose one's self and, in return, bring one closer to who they are."

"I don't say it, but you are special to me. Many years ago I was a different man, young and hopeful. A different man indeed. I was married." He paused for a long moment. "She was exquisite, but as a cop I couldn't give her the life she desired. She came from a family of wealth and luxury; she became pregnant. One night while I was on duty I got a call. The hospital admitted her. She had a miscarriage. I hadn't been there for her, instead I spent the night in the midst of a huge domestic battle involving firearms and injured innocent people. By the time I got to the hospital she'd vanished." His blue eyes distant. In his mind he was in the hospital with her all those years ago.

"The baby was a girl. She would be about your age. I buried her in San Francisco in a tiny coffin. She is the reason I've never left. I like being close to her. In my heart you share a place with her."

His stone exterior needed chiseling to break. Everyone owns

their secrets. La Tige hinted at his but refused details until now. I thought of Didier and how I left him at the altar, dissolving from his life forever. La Tige's passion and loss flowed through my heart. "I'm flattered. You're like the father I never had. You and Will are my family. Your wife… has she ever… " I fumbled for the right words, choosing La Tige bluntness. "What happened to her?"

"At first it was too painful. I grieved the daughter I would never know and my wife who abandoned us. Anger boiled inside me! Years went by and I made detective, a case took me close to her or part of her. When she vanished from the hospital her trail went cold. She ceased to exist." His blank eyes stared into the vast ocean.

"You've read my book. I did something similar. I left Paris the night before my wedding and came back to the States assuming the identity of Shanna Nu. That's when we met. I loved Didier but my past was too shady and I didn't know my own identity. How could I keep running from my past and live in a fantasy world with a husband who didn't know the *real* me? It didn't seem fair to him. I went back to Paris before settling in the Caribbean."

I paused for a second. My past was no secret to La Tige, but not my quick Paris trip I kept that secret. "I made a whirlwind trip to Paris and walked into the hotel. I wanted to say sorry for being a fool, enjoy the delight of his strong arms around me again, and hear him say everything was OK, he loved me regardless. But I realized that was a child's fantasy. I loved him but wasn't "in love" with him. I was a kid. He made my life with him a fairy tale. After years of searching I found my identity. I left a copy of my book on the concierge counter and jumped a plane to the

American mainland and finally the Virgin Islands."

I took a moment to formulate my next words. "Maybe she left to deal with her grief or escape a past like me and realized she was wrong to drag you into the twisted drama?" The romantic Puerto Rican music mimicked our conversation.

"Yes, she had a past, no woman that beautiful and exotic marries a man like me unless they are running." He stated, then deviated into the here and now. "I have a job for you if you're interested?"

The pound of the tide steady in the background, but our trip down memory lane and precious father daughter moment expired. Taken aback, I'm not sure how his mind shifted gears in just a few seconds. I stumbled over my words, making the transition. "I... uh... OK, what is the job?"

"I wouldn't ask, but I got a couple cases back home I need to close. The one I need you on has led me here, right here to PR. You must have read my mind when you booked this thing. An older couple visited me last week. Their son died of a heart attack and his widow sold his estate, took the money and vanished into thin air!"

His eyes met mine to make sure I followed his words. "It turns out the husband was a health nut and took a physical a few weeks prior to his death which showed his heart in absolutely perfect health. So how does a healthy guy die of a heart attack? And why does his wife disappear? You can understand why I took this case. His parents gave me a photo. I traced her - booked on a cruise here under an assumed name. The ship will dock here in three days. The next two, we will do whatever you want." His voice excited over the new case.

"Do you have her photo with you?" The wind whipped my French braid over my shoulder.

"Yeah, back in the room. I'll show you later. You interested?" He pushed my braid back to its spot behind my head.

"Yeah I'm interested! So my job is to find and observe her; take some inconspicuous tourist photos?"

He held my chin in his oversized hand, sincerity in his voice. "Yes, but be careful. If she murdered him she could be dangerous and I don't want you caught in the middle."

I looked into his sapphire blue eyes. "I understand, I can take care of myself, and I promise to be careful, you have my word."

With a chuckle, he said, "Yes, you can - better than any woman I have ever known - but careful isn't in your repertoire."

I leaned over and put my small arm around his wide back and my head on his shoulder. He reciprocated and gave me a kiss on the top of my head. The world stopped, and we shared a father and daughter moment on the beach. The tide now dangerously close to our feet.

At that moment in time, I believed my life mysteries solved, but deceit runs rampant in my genetics. My heritage is the spawn of evil spun out of control.

Play Time

I woke up in the morning to the unforgettable full-bodied aroma of Puerto Rican coffee. I had booked us into a two bedroom suite. As I drowsily sauntered out of my room I could see he was already up, sitting on the balcony which sported gorgeous views of the Atlantic. I poured myself a cup of coffee and sat down in the chair beside him.

"Morning. This is ass kickin' coffee!" he exclaimed.

Still half asleep, I responded, "That it is". I wasn't a huge coffee drinker but the coffee here was out of this world; it didn't even require sugar and cream to make it drinkable.

"I need to ditch my clothes and fill my suitcase full of it," he chuckled.

It was meant as a joke but I pictured him doing it and customs confiscating it.

He continued, "What's on the agenda for the day?"

"I booked us on a tour of the rain forest. It's unbelievable," I stated.

He looked at his clothes carefully and responded, "I didn't bring any hiking clothes".

Giggling, "They have tour buses, but you can hike if you want."

"What time is this tour?" he asked.

"Eleven o'clock." I retorted.

He bellowed, "We have time to eat then, I'm famished! Not much of "a morning person" are you?"

"Nope, never have been," I sluggishly responded, remembering the many times he would call me in the early hours when I worked for him.

He was up and ready so I finished my cup of coffee and showered, making myself presentable. We had breakfast at the resort. I had eggs and toast and he had the works - steak, eggs, potatoes, and more coffee. I drank more coffee as well while he finished. I wasn't much of a breakfast person either. Usually I ate more of a brunch.

The trip to the rain forest took a bit of time since it was on the east side of the island, but was fully worth it. The drive alone offered a landscape of flat topped homes and businesses open on all sides. The views from the top of the rain forest were impressive. Looking out from the top was a blanket of trees on all sides and we stood amidst the clouds. The animals blended so well into their surroundings that it took a keen eye to catch them. Amongst the waterfalls were pools of water surrounded by an elaborate framework of vegetation. The coquí sing the song of the rain forest. They are everywhere, but good luck trying to find one.

"Can't find sights like this in San Francisco!" he roared.

"Definitely not, I think it's one of the most amazing places on Earth." I agreed with a lively tone.

"Those frogs, what are they again?"

"The coqui."

He replied with a puzzled tone, "Yeah, they make quite a racket, but it's oddly relaxing."

"If you promise not to make fun of me," I gently jabbed him in the side, "I have a CD with rain forest sounds. When I'm having trouble sleeping, I listen to it and within a few minutes I'm asleep."

With a great, huge smile he said, "Do you dream of little frogs?"

"Occasionally," I answered in my most smart ass voice.

After the rain forest we ate a lunch-dinner combo. I had always been astounded by the amount of food he could pack into his gut. We ate in San Juan and the food was genuinely authentic. Resort food wasn't always the same quality and very overpriced. After, we meandered around and went into some of the shops. He bought coffee, surprise, and several different brands. My mind went back to my earlier vision of customs confiscating it. Well if they did I would have to mail him some. We caught a cab and headed back to the resort for drinks on the beach.

The following morning, I awoke once again to the luscious scent of coffee. I had planned a "man" day of deep sea fishing. We caught the boat just in time, and headed out over the blue vibrant waters while the crew explained all the ins and outs. It was a relaxing day and I was the only female. Even had I been interested, I couldn't have competed with fish;

although the captain had seemed to take an interest in me. He was local. I could tell by his accent, but he spoke English quite well. Most everybody involved in tourism did. He had thick, wavy brown hair that hung just below his shoulders.

As the day went on, his waves became tangles and he eventually put them into a ponytail with strands of curls that hung loose. His eyes were like dark chocolate fudge. He took his shirt off once we got out into the open ocean and his torso looked like a well carved statue; lined in muscles that extended to his shorts which hung just below his hips. He kept a close eye on me, ultimately making small talk.

His name was Raul and he was local, as I had suspected. Just a couple years ago he had purchased his boat and started chartering deep sea tours. He only worked with a couple of the resorts but hoped to buy more boats and work with more resorts eventually. I told him I was from St. Thomas and was here on vacation with a good friend. I didn't want to give him too many details. Before we departed he offered me his card and mentioned that he did private charters and I could call anytime.

As we walked away from the boat I could see La Tige was all smiles. He looked at me and said, "I think someone took a shine to you."

"You think? He gave me his card and told me to call anytime," I said, flashing the card in front of his square face.

"I'd say the feeling was mutual, you were lit up like a Christmas tree," he laughed out.

"OK, he was a really," I drug out the word really, "good looking guy and he was polite and maybe I'll call him sometime." I hadn't been too interested in finding a man. My past luck was not the greatest and Fetch had been the last one I'd seen during our little romp in New York.

"I'm ready to eat again; what do ya say?" he belted.

I was glad he changed the subject. I loved him but I wasn't too sure about offering details of my nonexistent sex life. We were both exhausted and ordered in - the wonders of room service. The last couple days had almost reminded me of my time in Paris. I loved the magic of the Caribbean. The crystal waters and pounding tide always brought memories, which really didn't make sense since I had never spent any time on the beach until moving here, but there was something here, something bewitching. I guess I a Tige had felt it too, as he shared with me how glad he was that I done this for him. He said, "Maybe one day I'll retire and move here. I haven't been this relaxed in decades!"

I unhinged my body from the comfort of the chaise and he snickered, "Hey Nu, no frogs tonight?" I was now legally Cleo, but he still called me Nu. Old habits die hard. I picked up the pillow positioned just below the rim of the chaise and threw it at him. As I tarried to the bedroom I heard him laughing.

Ashla

*I*t was a humid day and the sun was bright in the sky, but we were able to find a covered bench a distance from the port to sit on while we drank our coffee as we waited for the Black Widow to appear from the ship. La Tige pulled out his wallet and handed me a picture. I looked and gasped.

"This is her?" She could easily be my mother!

With no emotion he said, "That's her."

Flabbergasted, "You didn't notice how much she and I look alike?"

He took a long look at me and said, "I noticed." He took a long pause and continued, "Look at her features carefully. On a quick glance you look a lot alike but when you look closely its apparent she's probably had plastic surgery, Botox or something."

I looked more closely, "Her nose is too perfect, probably surgery."

"Look at her cheeks and the way her lips curl; I'm thinking a face lift or two," he replied.

"I see that and her eyes; she has no lines, not even joy lines. So she hasn't always looked this way. Could be the plastic surgery?" I replied begrudgingly. He noticed those details better than I and digital photography didn't hide much.

People flooded off the ship but she wasn't one of them and the heat of the sun was making me very uncomfortable. We waited and waited. We both thought we had seen someone like her but when we zoomed closer it was just another beautiful, dark haired woman.

"Hold on!" I grabbed my phone. It was top of the line and had an awesome camera. I zoomed in on her. "I see her, finally!"

He took a look at my phone, "Yup, that's her."

We watched her amble slowly and deliberately off the ship. She was obviously a woman that craved attention, especially that of the male persuasion. She flirted with the crew and smiled like a beauty pageant queen. Her teeth were so white they blinded my eyes even from the distance between us. We continued to observe safely tucked out of her sight.

A tall, hunky man met her at the foot of the off ramp. She swooned in his arms and they kissed, long and calculated on her part. Arms wrapped around each other they walked and talked, moving ever closer to us. As they walked past us I pretended to take pictures of La Tige but was really snapping pictures of her and her man. As soon as they had passed but were still within visual distance I showed him the pictures, "Could she possibly wear any more jewelry?" I asked, imagining her falling to the ground under the force of gravity from the weight of her jewelry.

"Her jewelry isn't all that's expensive, check out her bag and the quality of her clothes," he stated with little to no emotion.

"She likes money and I guess this guy is her new victim?"

"Looks like it. Come on, they are far enough away - we need to tail them," offered La Tige abruptly. Off we went, meandering after them casually.

They walked for a distance, which struck me as odd since she seemed more like the limo type, but eventually they entered a hotel. Not just any hotel but a very extravagant one. We sauntered in and sat in the lobby, out of sight but within earshot. We could hear them checking in. He introduced himself as Alberto Munoz Salazar and she as Ashla Cruz. Since he spoke with an accent I knew he was actually Spanish but she had no accent and spoke much punctuated English. We tailed them to their room and kept on walking and making small talk so we wouldn't stand out. Once they disappeared we went downstairs to the lobby.

"Nu, go ahead and check us out of the other place. I'm going to check you into this one under your alias Shanna Nu. I'll keep an eye on them and wait for you," he ordered. So much for his vacation. Now we were on the job. No use arguing.

When I got back to the hotel, La Tige was at the poolside bar having a leisurely drink.

"They ever reappear?"

"About half an hour ago, look to your three o'clock," said La Tige.

There they were, she in a bikini that had a couple of band aids over her chest and a string between her legs. Alberto couldn't take his eyes off her but neither could most of the men present at the pool. She was drinking a Piña Colada and he had something much simpler, beer, Medalla. He was a striking man, tall and lean. He appeared to be in his mid-thirties. On a quick glance she appeared the same age, even her ass and legs were taut. I wondered if there was surgery for that. Who was I kidding, of course there was. I'd seen the Kardashians on TV a couple times. She obviously took her appearance very seriously and flaunted it.

"I got you a room that looks into theirs. I tried getting you a room next to them or across the hall, nothing available, so I got you a room across from their balcony," he said and then handed me a couple small electronic gadgets.

Puzzled, I asked, "What are these?"

He responded, "This one," it looked like a computer chip, "is a GPS tracker and the others are cameras. You're creative. I'm sure you will find a way to plant them and use them. You can download their data straight to your phone, there's an app. I want you at a distance. Don't lose her. She could be dangerous. I got a couple hours before I catch my plane. Why don't you get cleaned up, I'll wait."

"You're right. I would love to sit and chat more with you but I feel gross and it looks to be a long night. You know... she didn't wait long did she?"

"Nope and I need to get home and research her past, everyone's got one, even those that want to hide theirs," he stated almost mournfully. Boy, did I have a past which La Tige knew all about.

As I sauntered to my room I couldn't help but notice how closely La tige watched her. He was at a distance but didn't let her out of his sight.

Finding my room was an adventure but it gave me time to decide where to put the GPS device. I had reasoned that the only item she probably never left behind was some type of cosmetic bag, a woman as vain as her wouldn't be caught dead without some way to primp herself at all times. I was a master pickpocket, so getting hold of her cosmetic bag for a few seconds wouldn't be too difficult. It would mean that I would have to get close enough to her momentarily to make it happen. I had decided that I would do it tonight.

The cameras I would worry about tomorrow when the GPS told me they were safely away from their room. I was also a master thief and jack of all guises. He had checked me in as Shanna, but Justine was more glamorous, so Justine I would be. To make my transformation complete I called and scheduled an appointment for tomorrow. It was no problem and they squeezed me in.

Before La Tige left he gave me a bear hug, truly not his style, and he said, "You be careful."

"I got it. I've danced with wolves before and they were my own family! I'll observe from a distance," I replied and then added, "If you can't get the coffee through customs I'll mail you some." I was half serious.

He replied with a belly roar, "I already thought of that and I left most of the coffee in the room." With that, he was gone. His behavior had been odd. He had been very affectionate and reminiscent this trip. We hadn't worked a case together in years. I mostly did remote clerical work. I even turned my smallest bedroom into an office. Logically, maybe this "Black Widow" brought back memories of his wife, but La Tige didn't run on emotion. I had to ask myself, *What was he like when he was married? Does he still love this woman?* I was curious and decided that I would track her down after our Black Widow case.

I slowly gathered information on Einstein's case as well. That is how I thought of it, all the young kids found dead, Einstein's case. I would solve it for him, one day. For now all I was doing was observing while he did the researching. I didn't even have my laptop. I could do most anything with my phone but had more access to data banks with my laptop. This I would have to do the old fashioned way because that is how he wanted it, otherwise he would have told me the purpose of his visit and I would have been prepared. Thinking to myself... *He didn't want me prepared... he is hiding something...*

Breaking and Entering

The couple drank merrily at the bar and I took a seat at a far table. Their choice of the bar over a table made my job easier, allowing a better visual. I waited for an opportunity.

"Mojito please," I asked the server as she came by.

As I sucked on my Mojito I kept a careful eye on Ashla's purse. She kept it dangling from the bar stool between her and Alberto. While waiting, I eavesdropped on their boring conversation, but their exaggerated mannerisms and confused speech told me they were tipsy. Soft Latin music matched the soothing sounds of the tide as it brushed along the shore.

Finally, Alberto got up and I seized the opportunity. I slipped in. Ashla's head turned opposite me, her purse wide open. Inside, near the top lay a small, salmon colored cosmetic bag, as I had suspected. I lifted the cosmetic bag, and placed it inside my rather oversized purse. She turned towards me. My heart jumped a beat.

"That seat is taken," she said.

"I'm just ordering a shot, I'll be out of the way as soon as I get the bartender's attention." I breathed a sigh of relief as she hadn't noticed my careful stash of her bag.

"Yes, they are very busy, let me help you," she said and shouted in the direction of the bartender, "Juan!"

A young dark haired man with bulging biceps jumped at his name and within seconds I held a straight shot of PR's finest rum.

"Thank you."

She smiled. Her skin taught around her lips from excessive facial reconstruction. I downed the shot quickly, leaving the glass on the counter, and walked towards the ladies' room where I locked myself into a stall and opened the bag. Her hotel key was stashed beside her compact. *Oh! Thank you.* I stashed it inside my own purse. She was making this easy for me. I continued to ransack the bag, searching for a place to slip the GPS device. The bag was impeccable and had no small tears so I took my trusty pocket knife, a purchase I recently made, and carved a small incision within the side of the bag. I worked the GPS device carefully into the lining and towards the bottom. I then left and returned to the bar before she noticed her lipstick was missing.

When I arrived, Alberto was seated beside her. I sauntered

towards the bar and shoved myself between them.

"Pardon, I couldn't help but notice your drink. It looks delicious, what is it?" I asked Ashla.

"It's a Piña Colada but they make a special recipe for me. Would you like to try one?" she asked with a notion of entitlement. I hated to be the person who stereotyped others, but she made it easy to envision her as a spoiled brat who'd had a sugar daddy in her pocket at all times.

"Yes, I would love one." I knew what she was drinking but the distraction offered me a chance to slip the bag back into her purse. She was so enthralled with herself that she never noticed my covert movements.

She and Alberto introduced themselves. I introduced myself as Justine.

"Isn't it the best?!" she exclaimed, her eyes green, brown,

hazel, I couldn't tell, were large and glowing with excitement.

"I don't know what the secret ingredient is, but it's absolutely to die for," I asserted as vivaciously as she. The truth was I didn't liked Piña Coladas and there were few things I didn't like; growing up on the streets I ate what I could get my hands on or dig out of the dumpster.

They continued to make small talk with me, but I didn't want to converse and really didn't want the drink, so I dug my cell phone out of my purse.

"I have a call, but it was nice to meet the both of you," I replied in a syrupy voice.

"Maybe we'll see you here tomorrow?"

I nodded my head and walked away, pretending to take a call. Then seated myself at a table parked next to a planter and inconspicuously fed my drink to the plant while I continued to fiddle with my phone. I engaged the GPS device with the app, soon after they left together. The device tracked their movements as I stayed seated. When they were safely in their room, I beelined to mine.

I strolled to my balcony scanning the balconies opposite mine, looking for theirs. It took a while but I found them. Their curtains drawn wide open and they were all over each other like butter on a warm biscuit. The bar below still packed with people and the Latin music drifted into the night air. The drunk couple soon passed out. I hadn't been that grateful in a while. My own bed beckoning me. Tomorrow was a new day.

Sunlight streamed through a crack in the curtains. Morning came too early. According to my GPS the lovers, Romeo and Juliet, were in their room. I quickly showered and dressed then padded towards the lobby. The aroma of fresh brewed coffee and bacon wafted from a restaurant off the lobby. It allowed a great view of the elevator. I ate light, lingering over every bite and sipped at my coffee. About an hour and three cups of coffee later, I felt as though I was becoming a coffee junkie like La Tige, they came downstairs and exited the hotel. They entered an awaiting car. The GPS would keep an eye on their location while I seized the opportunity to plant my cameras in their room.

The elevator doors swished open, I entered and smashed my finger on the third floor button. The doors slid closed and the elevator hummed, stopping unexpectedly on the second floor and an older couple entered. I heard the whine of a vacuum, so I slipped out. As I walked past the hotel maid's cart I spied what I needed. She had a box of latex gloves. Her back towards me as she vacuumed the floor, I grabbed a small handful and without missing a beat walked towards the elevator, and pressed the up arrow.

The third floor halls were empty. I approached their room with caution, glancing both ways, and the card slid easily across the door giving me a welcoming green light. I slipped inside and stuck the 'do not disturb' sign on the outside of the door and looked for a place to plant my cameras. Their room looked much like mine. The bathroom was to the immediate left with an oversized attached closet and a massive king size bed on the other side of the wall. The bed stared directly at a dresser with a vanity and next to that a large cabinet that contained a TV. Opposite the TV was a sitting area with a plush love seat and weird artwork above it. The balcony was beyond. I expected their room to be more extravagant, like a suite that carried a special name. Maybe she'd settled for not-quite-as-wealthy this time around.

After much contemplation, considering every angle I planted the cameras on the strange art above the love seat and on the top of the vanity. The camera above the vanity I angled towards the door. Satisfied I'd be able to see most everything I took a deep breath.

I searched their room, looking for clues. Digging through all their belongings and luggage and all I found was her expensive *call girl* wardrobe, several pairs of '*come and get me*' pumps and his clothes. In the bathroom she had enough beauty supplies to run her own day spa.

Inside the room vault I found jewelry that was pricey but not unique. A woman like her must have a more expensive collection somewhere. My GPS told me they were still far away, so I had time. I checked underneath and behind everything, opened all her bottles and potions but came up empty. *There had to be something here!* I snatched her suitcase and ran my fingers over every seam searching for hidden compartments and inconsistencies. Ready to throw up my arms in sheer frustration I found it! The moment was priceless.

There was a definite lump on the inside, behind a secret compartment! I carefully maneuvered my fingers around the edges. The seam was almost flawless, but there was a small disruption. I gently poked my finger into the hole and discovered the seam was velcroed. It contained a small red velvet bag which I pulled out. I dumped upside down on the floor, spilling its contents - six wedding rings. That is far too many husbands. Heck, I'd run at the thought of just one.

Five of the rings had huge rocks, large enough to gag an adult if swallowed, but one was a simple gold band. *Her collection!* I took photos that I could send to La Tige. The evidence supported the Black Widow theory. I placed the rings into the bag and pushed the bag inside the super hidden compartment. My fingers brushed against something else. It felt like small books. I pulled them out, *passports!* Six altogether and *Ashla Cruz* was not one of them. *That meant she had seven aliases! I thought I was extreme!* I took photos of each one. Then slipped the contents inside the compartment. I felt around one last time, satisfied that nothing else was hidden inside I put everything back how I had found it.

Confident the room didn't appear disturbed I applied the phone app to be sure everything worked properly and, as soon as I was satisfied, I exited the room.

Without a moment to spare I had just enough time to make my appointment and transformation back into Justine. I hadn't been Justine in nearly a decade which made it an even better cover. My physical transformation now complete, my hair sporting blond highlights throughout and trimmed at the ends and my fingers and toes freshly French manicured and pedicured with gel polish. Justine was well kept and wore nothing that wasn't of fine taste. There weren't too many fine French clothes to choose from, but I found a few outfits that would suffice.

It was now five-thirty and the love birds were still gone, according to my GPS they were in San Juan. My makeover complete and covert operation a success I called a cab. Time to catch up to Romeo and Juliet.

They were exactly where my device said they were, an outside bar and restaurant. From a distance, I kept an eye on them while I texted La Tige. He was home after his long flight. I had decided for the time being not to tell him about the rings and passports. He was hiding something and I wasn't sure what. All I knew was that for some reason this case was personal to him and he wanted me at a safe distance. *Was he afraid of what I would learn? If this lady is a "Black Widow" then why would she be dangerous to me?*

I needed to find out these answers and I needed items from my home. I called my new friend, chiseled-chest Raul, and asked him if he could charter an excursion to St. Thomas tonight. He agreed, big surprise there. I lived in a private community and we had a marina. My house wasn't a long walk from it.

I had two hours to kill before meeting Raul. Ashla and Alberto sucked at each other and flirted the time away and I watched as yet another man became nothing more than a huge diamond ring and paycheck.

Living in a Bad Movie

Raul was waiting when I arrived at the marina. He grasped my hand and helped me board his boat. The close proximity brought scents of aftershave and soap filling my nostrils. His aroma, along with the night ocean breeze, was intoxicating but I couldn't allow myself the distraction. I had will power since there was no history between us. My last excursion with Fetch breezed through my mind. I dismissed it and focused on the luscious man in front of me.

"I was surprised at your call," he said. His dark chocolate eyes flashing.

"I was surprised you could take me tonight."

With a smile that included a slight dimple on his left cheek he said, "Anything for a beautiful lady."

He was charming and glorious, even fully clothed. I handed him the directions and said, "You can wait at the marina for me. I won't be more than an hour." I wanted to give myself enough time, but would probably need only thirty minutes.

"Is no problem, there are some drinks in the cabin if you like?" he suggested. *Was he trying to get me drunk? Did I want to get drunk with him?* The outline of his round ass through his pants made firecrackers explode inside me.

"Thank you, maybe later. I like the water and watching the ocean part as the boat cuts through it. And the wind rushing against my skin." I also enjoyed watching him, but I kept that to myself.

His lips still parted in a smile, his eyes flashing over my tank top and cut-off denim shorts. "I don't get too many ladies travelling alone. Weren't you with an older man the other day?"

He hadn't said anything about my hair. It was dark out I told myself. "I was, a good friend, but he went back home."

"You're not worried to travel alone?" My travelling alone, I suppose, was strange; most people came here to visit with somebody or take a vacation with a loved one.

"No, I've travelled alone many times. I enjoy seeing the world." I didn't want to give him too many details. He was providing transportation and I was paying him well. He raked his fingers through his thick brown waves and started the motor.

Raul turned on the radio and I was glad for the relief in conversation. I considered slipping into the cabin below, but I relished the proximity between us. Sometimes life was an oxymoron. Now I had to combat the night ocean breezes, his arousing presence and Latin music! My brain and body were on overload. I checked my phone and saw the lovers had made their way to the hotel, where I was sure they'd stay.

Attempting to keep my mind off Raul, I counted boats. I didn't see many, a couple yachts passed by us and for a while a small two seater followed behind us. It veered off when the waters became rough. The boat probably couldn't handle the coarseness of the ocean. A large cruise ship loomed in the distance. My mind averted to sitting on the deck of the ocean liner with Raul and then, suddenly, Didier was beside me and they were arguing. Fetch strolled up to me, ignoring Raul and Didier and then Slug popped out of nowhere and shot them all dead. I shook my head, so much for fantasies. I was better concentrating on the here and now.

Approximately two hours later, and not a second too soon as my sensual desires for him were beginning to crown, we arrived at the marina. He helped me off and offered his assistance but I refused. *I needed to get away from him, not bring him to my home!* Who knows what would happen there! Visions of his body covering mine, the sand beneath us, going at each other like wild animals crossed my mind. I had to stay focused.

The walk to my house helped to center my mind and push the men in my life into an empty corner. I plunged my key into the lock and twisted. Home, my beautiful home. I didn't have time to linger, and plunge onto my comfy sofa. Down to business I checked my list and grabbed my flashlight, laptop and slipped it into its bag. I retrieved my binoculars that I used for watching ocean animals, and slipped those in the bag. Before leaving, I checked my phone, they were still at the hotel and there was no activity yet in their room. Now I was ready.

I swept the curtain aside and peered at the beach. My piece of Heaven. Then I turned on my heels and headed out the door. When I arrived at his boat he was laying on one of the seats at the stern. His shirt tussled above his pants which met just below his waistline. My eyes stopped at the chiseled V of his lower torso. He jumped when he saw me.

"Please, allow me," as he grabbed my bag. What a tantalizingly hot gentlemen. I liked him more by the second. *Get a grip!*

"Thank you."

The ride back, we talked about music. He not only liked Latin music but '90s rock! The same bands as me!

We talked on that subject for a while. He told me about his family. How he and his brother, Angel, ran the charter business. His parents and most of his family lived on the other side of the island. I wasn't sure what to say about my family so I only talked about William.

Raul slicked his hair into a pony tail, but a few stray curls hung loose, twisting in the wind. Didier had been the only man with short hair I'd ever been involved with. That struck me odd, as I had never thought I had a preference. *Maybe I did!* He docked his boat in PR and we continued to sit on it, drink beer and talk until the morning sun appeared. I kept my distance and attempted to make sure he kept his. No matter where I moved he moved closer. The heat radiating from him drove me wild. His chocolate eyes soaked in every clothed inch of my body.

My desire and need breaking down my will power I jumped from my seat as he scooted closer. "I gotta go, but thanks for taking the time," I said, not really wanting to leave but knowing I had to.

"I have no charters today, would you have dinner with me?" he asked, standing and moving closer to me. Jeez, he smelled sooo good, like man candy! I pushed the thought out of my head. It was simply my hormones, since I had lived like a nun since my last escapade with Fetch in New York.

"Can I call you?" I replied. His lips now only inches from mine. *What was I doing?*

"You call," he said. I bounced onto the steps before his luscious full lips met mine. I knew I'd be a goner and forget my mission if that happened. I grabbed my bag and slipped off his boat. Grabbing a taxi I headed to the hotel. My phone told me Ashla and Alberto were asleep, naked with the covers tangled between them. Exhausted, I lay in bed my mind thinking of Raul as I fell asleep...

The following morning, I set up my computer and checked in on Romeo and Juliet who were in their room all over each other again. I watched them but not too closely. In my sex deprived state I didn't need porn. I made coffee and plugged away at her aliases chronologically, starting with the most recent, Ashla Cruz. Since I had no passport, I didn't have much to go on except the name was different. All I found was an Ashla Cruz that died as an infant.

After hours of researching databanks, I found all the others had also died as young children or infants. Ashla and lover boy were still at it. *Didn't they ever take a break?* All her aliases had death certificates! If they had lived they would all be between the ages of thirty to forty. There was one more name, but first I was curious about Alberto Munoz Salazar, the boyfriend.

She came here to see him and their body language with each other was more like long time star crossed lovers than new lovers. Maybe they work as a team and he's not a victim. His name was like looking for a needle in a haystack! There were hundreds of death certificates and marriage licenses. So I cross referenced the name with her identities. I found nothing in connection with any of her names. *Is Alberto his real name? Is he a victim?* I must have found a couple hundred in Puerto Rico alone.

Frustrated, I decided to run her locations, according to the passports, against his name. *Bingo!* I found they had been in several locations together over the past fifteen years. My mind raced! *He is her lover and partner?* She seduces the men, spinning them into her web and Alberto does the killing! I emailed La Tige with my research. My next step was to cross her aliases with marriage licenses and then dates, but for now my body was stiff and my mind was on overload.

I stood and stretched my stiff arms. Sitting in front of my computer for hours my entire body felt like petrified wood. The lovebirds were still at it. *I could make a fortune off videotaping them!* I'd be the next Hugh Hefner, but in female form. Watching them was like living in a really bad porn movie, the type with no plot just a lot of sex! I decided I couldn't take watching them anymore and pondered all that I had learned.

I plucked Raul's card off the bedside table, flipping it between my pointer and index fingers. He wanted to take me to dinner. *Why not?*

Who's There?

Raul took me through old San Juan. The charm of the city was enticing. Or maybe it was his charm. He opened doors for me, pulled out chairs then scooted them once I sat down. Everywhere we went was a party. We ate, he taught me Latin dance moves. His hips gyrating in sync with mine. I drank a Mojito at every stop. The streets were filled with life and music. He knew the city well and the coolest spots.

It was our third stop when the alcohol caught up to my bladder. On my way to the restroom I noticed a tall, salt and pepper haired gentleman watching me. He stuck out because he was dressed in a suit like he was a lawyer or stock trader;

everyone else was dressed casually or wearing party clothes. He looked to be about sixty-ish. When he saw that I noticed him he smiled at me. *Weird!* He was far too old for me. I much preferred men my age. I shook the creepy feeling from my head and when I came back out he was gone. Relief washed over me and I realized maybe I was paranoid. He was probably waiting on his wife or girlfriend.

In the bathroom, I checked my GPS and code names Romeo and Juliet were on the move. In fact they were heading my way. *Good!* I could watch them and play with Raul at the same time. I kept the app open for easy access and slipped my phone into an inside pocket of my purse.

A young couple sat at the table with Raul. He introduced me. They were friends of his. I hadn't even thought about that, I bet he knows a lot of people local to the area.

We stayed with the other couple, Cecelia and Felipe, for a while. Cecelia had dark skin with black silk eyes. Her dress hugged each curve of her body. Waves of thick hair covered Felipe's head and sprung in every direction. He spoke Spanglish with a thick accent, moving my chair out before Raul got the chance. *Are all men in Puerto Rico gentlemen?*

I checked inside my purse and Ashla and Alberto were here. I looked around but didn't see them. *Where were they?* I excused myself, saying I left my lip gloss in the bathroom and sauntered to the restroom. It was there I ran into Ashla, admiring herself in the powder room mirror, her makeup bag lying on the counter. I thought of the device I stuck inside it. She had a knack for hiding things too. I tried to sneak past her but she was too observant, "Justine, right? We met the other night."

"Yeah, nice to see you again, small world." I was beginning to wonder if my hair color made any change in my appearance or if it was just my imagination.

"You must have a drink with us!" she boomed, her greenish eyes flashing.

"I would love to, but I'm here with a date." I responded, hoping she would give up.

"Him too." Oh, whoppee!

I smiled and hoped she would be gone when I was done in the restroom. She was too friendly, especially for a Black Widow with a sociopathic boyfriend. Remembering she too had a knack for hiding items within seams, I dug through my own purse looking for any discrepancies. With a sigh of relief I found none, maybe it was sheer coincidence that they were here. *Heck most of San Juan is here tonight.* Her heels tapped across the tile floor and the door creaked open. She was gone.

Strolling towards Raul, Ashla blindsided me. She took my arm and walked with me like we were old buddies or something. From this close to her I saw the blemishes in her face. Areas looked to be smoothed, like with a rolling pin, to get rid of any lines and wrinkles. A few gray hairs poked from her roots, but it could have been the reflection from the lights making the hairs appear gray. She rattled on about how beautiful the night was and how I should introduce her to my date. It appeared I was stuck with her. *Who did she think she was?* My job was to monitor her not be her new BFF but right now I didn't have a choice.

Latin music filled my ears and a light, sensuous breeze blew intermittently. At the table she introduced herself to everyone and waved Alberto over. *She took over my beautiful evening!* The anger inside me rose. *I don't want her here! I don't want Raul and his friends having drinks with psychopaths!* Alberto bought rounds of drinks for all of us. Everybody but me welcomed them and enjoyed a good time. From the corner of my eye I thought I saw the salt and pepper haired man again. *I needed to get out of here.*

When I saw the opportunity, I grabbed Raul and ran towards the beach, getting away from her. She was too nice and gave me the creeps. It wasn't her personality but her doppelganger-me appearance which incidentally also reminded me of my bio-mom who I wanted nothing to do with. Once we reached the sand I yanked off my sandals, falling backwards onto my bum. I had indulged too much alcohol. Raul took my hands and lifted me to my feet. We strolled across the beach, the water skimming our feet and sliding up our ankles. Elated from the alcohol I stopped, looked at the ocean and allowed the wind to catch my hair, whipping it across my face. "Can you feel the breeze? Sometimes at home, I stand in front of the ocean like this and allow the wind to carry my thoughts away."

"I like the wind too and the ocean, my favorite place to be on nights like tonight is on my boat. There I can be one with the wind and ocean," he stated, his hair floating across his face from the breeze. I caught glimpses of his dimple and his chocolate brown eyes were nearly covered by waves of dark hair. *He would make beautiful babies*, I pondered. *Holy crap! I was lost in that moment and what on Saturn was I thinking*!

He caressed the hair from my face and kissed my cheek working his way towards my mouth. The touch of his lips soft against mine. His tongue curling against mine. I allowed myself to get lost in that moment.

He pulled his lips off mine and ran his tongue over them. "I like you, you are different and beautiful. You are like a hibiscus. They are the most attractive flower in bloom. They bewitch the humming birds with their bright colors. You are like a hibiscus in bloom and I am a hummingbird, that couple, the ones from your hotel they are humming birds too. When a hibiscus drops, they look like butterflies and I imagine them flying away. I don't know where you come from and one day you may fall and spread your wings to fly off like a butterfly," remarked Raul in a melancholy tone.

That was possibly the most sentimental statement anyone had ever said to me and he was right, I always spread my wings and flew off like a butterfly but now I had a home, my home. "I'm not going anywhere this time…" my voice trailed off.

He cupped his hands around my face and parted my lips with his tongue. I closed my eyes to feel the full effect of his tongue joyriding in my mouth and sending shivers of pleasure up and down my spine. My mind drifted to Fetch and how lost and clumsy I got when he kissed me. I'd lose all bearings and become a female sex puppet. Raul had that same effect on me. When I opened my eyes his chocolate browns were looking deeply into my emeralds, searching for something. Deciphering my feelings possibly, or hoping my female hormones would invite him up to my room. *Will power! I wasn't yet ready for more than the beautiful moment we shared.*

At the hotel he said goodnight and gave me another kiss. I wandered to my room in a daze. My mind wasn't foggy enough for me to not notice the man again outside the hotel. I simply didn't care. If he was following me than I hoped he had a good show. I rested my head on my pillow, closed my eyes and fell into a very deep sleep.

When I awoke my head felt like an elephant was standing on it! In slow motion I lifted it up, attempting to orient myself. My purse was on the floor beside me and I was fully clothed, shoes and all! I picked up my purse, holding my head with one hand and checked my phone - nothing. The battery was dead! I had left the app on and it drained it! Carefully steadying myself on my own two feet, I grabbed my charger and plugged in my phone. Then I went to the room phone and ordered a huge breakfast - the works, eggs, bacon, pancakes and potatoes. I had found the best way to get rid of a hangover was to starch it up.

Caribbean Heat Baby Girl V

After breakfast, I brought my computer to my bed where I planned on staying all day. I checked my phone and had one text message from Raul, *I had a good time, I hope to see you again.* He was perfect, which worried me a little. I always found perfect men and then something happened. *Sometimes that something was me.* No messages from La Tige. I checked my email and no messages there either. *That was strange?* I checked on Alberto and Ashla. They were not in their room, so I checked the GPS and they were still here in the hotel.

All Ashla's identifications were from dead people, *were mine?* I hadn't known my true identity until I was nearly twenty-one and then I changed it for good, legally! It felt good to be me, to know who I was. Ashla had spent her life changing to cover up who she was.

I labored at my computer investigating all my aliases, including what I thought for first two decades of my life was my birth name. They were all from dead people! All of them were like Ashla's, girls who had died young!

I was beginning to see similarities between us. I had thought I was protecting myself and searching for who I was, but I was also running from my past. *Is Ashla running or hiding? Is she, like me, a victim?* An idea began to formulate in my mind.

Following my leads from yesterday and my new hypothesis, I cross referenced all variables I could think of. All of her aliases had marriage licenses to men who were deceased. All her husbands died in different ways, which included natural causes and horrible accidents. *There was no exact method except they were all dead*! She had collected insurance on every one of them and liquidated all their assets shortly after their deaths, making her a very wealthy woman!

Her husbands had a lot in common, besides being dead. They were all relatively young and had six figure incomes. All this pointed to her being guilty, but I couldn't shake the idea that she was a victim not a murderess. Maybe she acted the part well or maybe it was the connection I was beginning to feel towards her, but my gut said she was innocent. All her meetings with Alberto were after the death of a spouse - again this implied guilt. She beguiles men and they unknowingly walk into her snare, where Alberto does his handy work. Next they spend a few sordid weeks together looking for a new patsy. I still hadn't researched her first identity but it would have to wait.

Downstairs in the lobby I stopped in for a very late dinner. My attention fully concentrated on the case. I was caught off guard by a distinct and strongly accented voice, "May I sit?" It was the salt and pepper haired man from the night before!

Blood is Thicker than Water

Startled, my eyes the size of saucers I stammered, "I prefer to eat alone."

"Please, ah... I notice you are breathtaking," he sputtered out, deeply Middle Eastern accented.

"Really, I'm not interested. I prefer men closer to my age."

He laughed, "I see you with a... a... man last night. Yes, your boyfriend?"

"I've had enough," I stood, ready to walk off.

"Please," he said and touched my shoulder. He pulled out a picture and handed it to me. It was old and worn but holy shit it looked like me! He continued, "You look much like this woman?"

"There is a resemblance, who is she?"

"My sister, when I saw you I thought you were her but she is ah… now older ah… picture was taken when she was sixteen."

I studied the picture. Everybody has a twin and I thought mine was my birth mother until I met Ashla, but this woman looked like me too, on initial examination. As I looked more closely at her features I immediately knew who she was! My interest was piqued.

"Yes, I know who she is. You didn't see her last night?"

"It was a… ah… crowded. I saw you."

I felt badly for the man. I knew what it was like to search for my own roots and find that I have siblings I hadn't known existed. "OK, we'll make a deal before I tell you anything or help you. I have a few questions.

You answer them and I will lead you to her, OK?"

"Yes, OK, is fair," he said, his voice shrouded in hope. He took a seat at the booth across from me.

According to him, she disappeared shortly after being married. She was his youngest sibling. He was the oldest of four other siblings. They all shared the same father but had two different mothers, his mother being different than hers. His sister's name was Aaliyah. It had been arranged for her to marry and, as arranged, she was married at seventeen. Her husband made a modest living and could take good care of her. *Aaliyah, Aaliyah, Aaliyah. The name bounced across my brain. Why was it familiar?*

One and a half years after being married, she disappeared. His father told him not to search. As his son, he respected his request, but when their father died six years ago he decided to find her. His family had money and resources which led him here. To him it was necessary to explain how in his country, many men take on more than one wife, provided they can care for all their wives and children equally. I was old enough to understand each country had customs and it was not for me to judge them. My own bio-father wasn't married to my bio-mom, he was a sperm donor and she a uterus donor. He was also compelled to explain that she was their father's only daughter and he had deeply loved her.

This man bore his heart to a stranger, me, with sincerity in his voice. It was my turn to live up to my end of the bargain. It was time to take him to her. "I'm going to lead you to her, but you can't ask how I know you and you need to play along."

"I have told you much, please, are you her... her... daughter?" he asked with caution.

"What! No, no! My mother died when I was twelve. The woman who raised me died when I was twelve. My bio-mom is very much alive, but not here. That is all I will tell you. Let's reunite you with your sister."

"Your mother did not raise you?"

"I already said that is all I will tell you! You have told me about your family because you want to find your sister. My family is of no concern to the situation," I stated very bluntly.

He, his name David, his tone and body language genuine. I knew exactly where she was and guided him straight to her. Since my new BFF acquisition last night, she would not find it odd. They were relaxing by the pool. "Ashla?" I interrupted her sun baking time. *If she spent this much time in the sun how did she not have leather skin by her age?* I was perplexed.

She sat up, startled, and stared towards David. "Justine, who..." her voice trailed off.

I interjected, "Meet my new friend, David."

Alberto sat up, his eyes slanted with curiosity, and said, "Hello David, nice to meet you."

Ashla looked dumbfounded and clearly unsure who David was, but I read partial recognition on her face. I looked at Alberto. "Would you mind getting us a round of drinks?" I asked in a cinnamon-sugar voice. Unsure of the situation he provided me with a stern face before getting up and walking towards the crowded bar.

"Please, this is not the place, come with me," I said as I walked towards the hotel beach bar and restaurant. At a quiet table near the shore I said, "Please sit, David meet Ashla, Ashla meet David. I think the two of you have something to discuss and it's personal. I'm going to find Alberto and we'll catch up later."

David, with an extremely puzzled expression, asked "You are leaving?"

"For now." *Did he want me around for the entire family reunion?* I'd had my own in New York and wasn't interested.

I found Alberto ambling towards me with a scowl of fear and male ego "white knight" syndrome on his face.

"Where is she?!"

"She's fine, look towards the beach." I pointed towards the long lost siblings.

"I don't think you understand. She shouldn't be alone with him!"

"So why don't you fill me in over those drinks you're carrying?" I insisted, grabbing his arm and guiding him towards the bar. Ashla and David needed a few minutes of peace.

He shoved the drinks at me and ran down the beach. Chunks of sand flying as each foot lifted. *Men!* I followed.

At the table, Ashla assured Alberto everything was fine and he should have drinks with me. Reluctantly, he scowled off with his tail between his legs. Speaking towards me, "You have explaining to do, now!" *Can we say overprotective pit-bull?*

I sat with Alberto and we made use of the drinks. He continued to order round after round and we talked. The server made rounds every ten to fifteen minutes. He grew more and more drunk with each drink. My job was to observe from a distance not implant myself into the center of their lives. *How would I explain this to La Tige?* I didn't come to them. They came to me, but it didn't matter. I felt compelled to assist them and even I didn't understand why. Maybe because David seemed so nice and I really didn't believe Ashla or Alberto were serial killers or because Ashla's oldest passport shared the same last name as my birth mother. The same last name as my own birth certificate. But it was a common name in some parts of the world. The name was Laila Shariff, but that was not her real name. David said her name was Aaliyah so Laila Shariff was obviously a fake, probably taken from another young dead girl. The common name was the reason I had put off finding its roots. A part of me didn't want to know.

The drunker he got, the more he opened up, but his speech had become slurred. Ashla and David still sat on the beach, the sun now fully set, and I listened to Alberto ramble. I was able to piece together that her first husband was an abusive indignant who treated her as a punching bag. He took sex whenever he wanted it. She had escaped all that with the help of her father. Over the years, her first husband had hunted her and every time he found her, death followed.

So now I understood all her aliases but I still didn't get why she had married so many times or why she hadn't married Alberto. They had been lovers for a decade and a half. The question lingered on the tip of my brain. He wouldn't remember much in the morning and he was flowing like a broken water main. "Alberto, why did she always remarry? Why not marry you?" He looked at me like that was the most obvious answer on Earth.

"She loves me."

Well cornhuskers, why hadn't I thought of that? Because it made perfect sense not to marry the man you love. I was beginning to see even more resemblance between Ashla and myself. "I get that but why not marry you instead of other men?"

"If she had married me, I would surely be dead by now," he stated, as if those other men's lives were somehow less important than his.

"But what about all those other men?"

"She thought each time she could hide. She used the money and changed her appearance in some way. She'd make herself into a new person, but it didn't matter, he always found her. She travelled to every continent and he always found her." *That explains all her facial reconstruction.* His eyes fixed on his drink, he ran his thumb over the rim of the glass. "I was a very young man when I met her... She wants a life, a real life. Her life was stolen from her by an evil man. I would marry her, but she won't have it."

"She doesn't want you to die," I stated the obvious. I also got the obvious connection between her and myself. I had done pretty much the same thing, only I never got married or did something I knew would get someone killed. There was the Halette incident but it was self-defense. Now I got it. She and Alberto were not murderers or serial killers or psychopaths. They were the victims of a psychopath!

"Can we go back for a minute? You said that her father helped her escape her first husband. Did he continue assistance over all these years?"

"Yes, until he died."

"Six years ago?"

"Yes."

I had to ask. The name coincidence, our physical resemblances, and our fateful decisions fraught with agony were too compelling. "Where did he hide her when he first helped her escape?"

"I think with her sister," he replied in short.

"She doesn't have a sister, according to David."

"He wouldn't know. She is a half-sister. Her father had a family in America too, and a daughter. He enjoyed women and he took care of them. He had a girlfriend in New York; I think her name was Camille? They had two daughters, Celia and Laila, but Laila died in infancy. Her father gave her Laila's name and sent her to America to live with Celia. Celia is a few years older." *I was named after my bio-grandmother?*

"Celia Shariff?" I faltered, dumbfounded.

"How do you know that?" he questioned, his eyebrows squinted in a V.

My brain reeled in all directions as it soaked in all the information. I had been drinking soda, but I grabbed his rum and coke and sucked it dry. "I need another drink, do you?"

"Sure." The server whizzed past us and he ordered two more drinks.

"The world grows smaller each and every day. Your girlfriend's half-sister is my birth mother." I stated. He had told me everything. I was compelled to return information and I needed to talk with someone who was as absorbed as me in the secrets of my family.

"I know. You were named after your grandmother."

"So you knew! You knew as you explained to me that your girlfriend is my half-aunt! Why not just say something from the get go?" Anger bubbled inside me like an erupting volcano.

"Do you think I would have told you anything if I hadn't already known your history? I love Ashla. I would never do anything to bring her harm. I have never told a soul what I just told you and I only told you because I knew you are her sister's child!"

"OK, calm down!" I raged, spiking my feathers. "Sometimes it is nice to talk with someone openly, no holds barred." My anger subsided.

"And I'm going to fill you in on another secret so long as you promise not to run away." he snuck in using a "be good" tone with me and flashing the evil eye my way.

"There's more?" *How could there possibly be more?* Soon I would have to make a chart of all my bio-people and send it to ancestry.com.

I shook my head and he glowered at me. "Fine, I promise," I said, not hiding my sarcastic tone.

"A real promise, if you run she will know I told you. She and her sister are very close. They are the only family each other have so you can't leave or let on that you know." Sincerity hung on the edge of his words.

I looked at him and read his eyes as sincerely as my drunkenness allowed, I responded, "I promise I won't leave and I promise I won't say anything to anyone."

"Celia will be here in two days."

"Celia what?! Why? To see me! The woman who let me rot with a junkie for twelve years, that junkie was more of a mother than she could ever be!"

"Calm down, people are looking," he said. I took a deep breath. He continued, "Celia is not like Ashla. She is more fragile. It is taking a lot of courage for her to come here. She knows what you must think of her, but she has spent twenty-two years waiting to meet you. You met your father and your brother and sisters, maybe she is worth giving a chance?"

I wrapped my hands around my head. "I'm not going to run," I said, unwrapping my head. Looking into his eyes, I advanced, "It's harder for me to accept her because she is my mother, biologically. I come here thinking my past is my past and my life is now a clean slate but I'm wrong. My past and family is always blowing up at me. I can't run from it."

La Tige?

Still no answer. Now I'm worried. Celia - who cares, she will have to wait! I don't have time for her. La Tige and San Francisco can't wait. He was the man who stood by me, loved me, cared for me. I sat on my balcony, worried and upset. La Tige doesn't always respond right away but he always gets back to me and it's been days since I emailed him and no response. I tried calling and nothing. His phone goes to voicemail. This man had been more a parent and friend than anyone else I know and my gut was telling me something was wrong. My belly butterflies flopped like rabid raccoons. I booked a flight to St. Thomas to go home and drop everything off. I was not coming back here! After St. Thomas on to S.F., I was going to find him!

It was good to be home! My little piece of Eden, but there was no time to revel in it. I dropped everything inside me bedroom and packed a new bag; my flight was leaving in ninety-seven minutes and I had to be on it! My mind thinking many awful scenarios such as La Tige hunted by the psychopath husband, bound and tied, beaten to a pulp, or La Tige lying in a ditch, bloody with stab wounds!

On the cab ride to the airport I gave Kacy a call. I knew she'd be happy to see me and maybe we'd have time to talk. I needed my best friend right now.

"Cleo, what's up?" Her voice sounded like syrupy, chocolate-covered strawberries.

"I'm going to be in San Fran for a few days."

"By the sound of your voice, this isn't a pleasure, let's-hang-out kind of trip." She knew me well, too well, and read my mind through my voice over the phone.

"I haven't been able to get hold of La Tige. He's got this weird case that I'm helping him with and he hasn't answered his calls. I'm worried. He's tough and hard on the outside but soft and sweet inside."

"You just described a Three Musketeers candy bar. His office isn't far from the bar. I'll make a quick stop. Look, I'm sure he's fine. It wouldn't be the first time he didn't respond right away to a phone call." Kacy tried to comfort me and soothe my anxiety.

"No! Kacy this is dangerous, more dangerous than he thought. I couldn't handle both of you missing!" My anxiety was cresting and moistness took over my eyes, threatening to let loose.

"Doesn't he have any cop friends?"

I hadn't even thought of that. "Officer Han was his ex-partner."

"Sweetie, relax. I got this."

"I'm at the airport, please don't go by his office. Promise?" Worry, fear, and loads of anxiety had cropped up, slowly consuming my body.

Kacy paused for a second or two. Too many seconds. "Kacy, promise?"

"I promise. Love you. When's your plane land?"

I gave her the flight and arrival time and we hung up, but not before I said, "Love you too!"

On the plane I tried to calm my mind and decipher a plan. First, I would go by his office. I had a key and I would let myself in and search for any clues on his whereabouts. Maybe I was worried over nothing as Kacy suggested and he was unavailable because of a case he was working. He said he had things to take care of. I had to think positive *La Tige is OK, La*

Tige is OK. My heart would drop out of my bottom and I would wither away if anything happened to him.

Next, I would go by his house. If he had been home anytime recently I would be able to tell. He wasn't the tidiest of people and there would be "telltale" signs whether he had been home or not such as Chinese leftovers and burrito wrappers. Hopefully, I would find some clue at his office or home but if not I could always call Officer Han. They had been partners and were still friends. Now with some type of plan, the butterflies in my belly felt more at ease.

My mind wandered and Raul with his carved statuesque torso barreled to the front giving me a sudden epiphany; *Raul had been extremely eager to get to know me and cozied up to Ashla and Alberto the previous night, laughing and joking like they were old buddies. Was he somehow part of someone else's bigger plan for me?* He can't be the serial killer, he is too young. OK, there wasn't an age that one becomes a serial killer. Maybe he is a hired killer to get close to Ashla. Maybe her serial killer husband doesn't do the killing himself. Could it be he hires people? At this flash of thought I was happy that I had not taken him to my house the night he took me to St. Thomas.

This plane wasn't moving fast enough and my flight wasn't direct, I had a stop in Orlando before continuing on to S.F. At this moment I wished I could transport. *Beam me up Scottie!*

Orlando was a quick stop. I literally ran from one gate to the next, pushing my way through the crowds and vendors. My seat was a welcome sight! I'd been jet-setting for years but had the strange habit of still tucking my purse beneath my seat around one of my legs. Old

habits die hard and I was unusually
full of anxiety at the moment.

Back to the Bay

I turned my phone on as we landed in San Francisco and texted Kacy *here*. She texted back *outside waiting.* I couldn't wait to see her! Anxiety left me for the moment, being replaced with excitement. I pushed through the crowds and waltzed out the door.

It was a windy day as I walked out of the airport and cold. I wasn't used to cold, dry weather but luckily I had packed a jacket. I put my bag on a bench and rifled through till I found it. The moment I crammed one arm into an armhole I heard Kacy's voice. Sure as she said, Kacy waited outside, circling the airport pick up zone. She greeted me with a huge hug and the words, "Sweetie, we need to go!"

No formalities just *we need to go. Why was she in such a rush? Was she sensing my anxiety?* It didn't matter. She was right, we needed to get on the road and drop my stuff at her place so I could get to La Tige's office ASAP. "Let's go."

In the car, Kacy's eyes on the road, she dropped a nuclear bomb, "Don't get upset." Anything that starts out with *Don't get upset* would be something that is definitely going to upset me.

"What did you do?" I asked, with apprehension knowing exactly what she did but wanting to hear it from her.

"I didn't go by La Tige's office if that's what you're afraid of. I sent Big Billy by his office." Big Billy was a Happy Trails bar patron that might as well have stock in the bar. He was there every day, like a Norm from *Cheers*.

My guts twisted inside and fear rose up through my chest into my vocal chords. "What did Big Billy find?"

"La Tige wasn't there and his office was a mess."

The fear in my vocal chords sunk back into my stomach and dissipated. "His office is always a mess and he's rarely there."

"Not a usual La Tige mess but a-tornado-rolled-through-his-office mess."

The fear shot through me again. "Like an F5 tornado messy or an F2 messy?"

"F9!"

"There is no such thing as an F9 but I get your drift." My body was in fear's grasp. It dominated me more than I could ever remember it - even worse than when I lost Einstein.

Tears soaked my eyes and blurred my vision but I could see we were clearly not on the way to Happy

Trails, Kacy's bar. "Where are we going?"

"To La Tige's office, where else?" Kacy said this as if I expected it. I had told her not to get involved. I couldn't lose both of them in one day!

"No, no, no. You need to get back to the bar. You can't come with!"

"Oh yes, I can. You are the best friend I've ever had and I'm not letting you walk into danger alone. I have weapons of mass destruction. OK, not mass destruction, but we can do some harm if anyone messes with us." She said this with a confidence, which made me curious what type of weapons she had accumulated during the past several hours I had been in the air.

"Like?"

"Nothing that will kill anyone but something that will incapacitate them uncomfortably for a while, long enough for us to run for our lives."

I looked at her pensively, narrowing my eyes. "What does that mean, exactly?"

"Tear gas, honey." She must have felt my eyes drilling into her head because she continued and reached, looking for a reason to come with me.

"I read your book, remember? You faced life alone, on the run. Well you're not alone anymore and I want a piece of the action. We can so do this!" Her voice gave away her longing for excitement and her love for me. I didn't have a choice. She was coming whether I liked it or not and that was Kacy. I had to respect it and get hold of her can of tear gas. My mind imagined her spraying it but instead of the bad guy she got us and we spent hours puking uncomfortably.

"I get it. It would be nice to have a partner in crime." The thought brought back Einstein and our crime spree days, but those days were over. Bring on *Thelma and Louise*, ditch *Bonnie and Clyde*.

I felt my phone buzzing and yanked it out of my pocket with quickness. It was a message from La Tige! Finally! The message read, "Everything is good. Sorry I didn't get back to you. I've been working a case." *Nothing else? No questions about Ashla?* Almost too many words in that message. Not like him. He would have said something simpler like: *All's good been working case.* Why suddenly send the message now when I was clearly not in PR anymore. I needed to get to his office right away!

"Who is it?" asked Kacy, anticipation strong in her voice.

"La Tige..." I took a moment to collect my thoughts. "It was his phone but I don't think it was him. Too many words." We both sat quiet for a few minutes before Kacy steered the car off the next exit and we tore through the city. The car ripping up and down the streets as Kacy's lead foot dodged any obstacles; cars, buses, and people.

After a hellacious ride, one that normally would have made my stomach queasy, Kacy squealed her car into his parking lot and slammed the car into gear yanking the keys out of the ignition in one fluid movement.

"Hold on. We need a plan. We can't go in halfcocked. Where is the tear gas?"

She pulled a silver canister out of her purse and handed it to me. I dared not ask where she got it. Be sure you pull this red tab," she said, pointing to a red plastic piece near the lid of the canister. "Make sure it's pointing away from you. You don't want to spray yourself, or me." Evidently she had the same fears I did. "One more thing - cover your face and spray as far as you can."

"That was two things, but I got it. I'm going first. Stay behind me a safe distance." I had to protect my friend. I also had better self-defense skills than Kacy.

We snuck upstairs to his office. I slid my key in the door, listening for the click that told me the door was unlocked. The sound never came. The door was already unlocked. I whispered to Kacy, "How did Big Billy get in?"

"I didn't ask. I thought maybe he looked through the frosted glass."

"The door was unlocked. He didn't mention that?"

"He might have. My mind was thinking of what tools I needed and how exactly I was going to talk you into bringing me with you."

"Jeez Kacy, really?" She gave me a cheesy smile.

I listened at the door and there was no noise coming from the office. He wouldn't have left the door unlocked. Someone had been here, but now they were gone. We had no weapons except a small can of tear gas. I took it out, pulled my shirt over my face and nose and motioned Kacy to do the same. I placed my fingers on the tab and pulled carefully with the trigger pointed in the opposite direction of us, just in case. My finger now cautiously above the trigger, the canister in front of us, I stood beside the door and gently kicked it open.

Nothing, I peered inside and saw no one. The F5 tornado mess stared at me. Files lay everywhere. Cautiously, I moved into the office signaling Kacy to stay outside. I wandered towards my old desk. At this moment, memories swept over me as I remembered sitting in the comfy rolling chair searching for information that would lead me to the answers from my past. I ran my finger across the chair and spun it around, embracing my memories of such a troubled and mysterious previous life. Here I was again, shrouded with the skeletons of my family's past and the whereabouts of a man whom I had come to love. I shook the flashback from my head and made my way through the office.

There was no one here and no sounds. Kacy peered around the door and I motioned her in. "What are we looking for?"

"I don't really know. I expect it will jump out at me when I find it. Clues always do." I set down my canister and rifled through his desk, looking for breadcrumbs, anything that would tell me where he might be, where he might have gone. Files stacked in sloppy piles and several boxes packed covered the floor. I had just realized this. *Boxes? Why? Is he planning on moving his office?* This had been his location since he quit the force. *Why would he move now?*

I stepped over the piles and haphazard stacks on the floor to his desk. Sifting through the mess I found his calendar buried under files on his desk. The day after he got back from PR he had a meeting scheduled at his favorite dive. No clues as to who he was meeting or why. It could be something simple like meeting a friend or complex like meeting a client. He was the epitome of what one might expect of an ex-cop now turned P.I. He was a true cliché.

I looked up and caught movement in the hallway from the corner of my eye, the door was wide open. I cursed under my breath for being so sloppy as to forget to not only close the door but lock it too. I stopped and listened with my keenest ear. Kacy's eyes grew huge as space ships. She heard it too, a slight movement, footsteps?

Then I heard nothing, silence. I grabbed the canister of tear gas and pulled my shirt back over my nose and mouth. Kacy had one as well, pointed directly towards the door. *What?* Not only one but she has two. This wasn't the moment to worry about it. I'd get onto her later. We both stood only feet from the door, our canisters pointed in its direction, and with that I felt a pin prick in my neck, like a bee sting and I sprayed the canister as I heard a thump beside me then everything went fuzzy...

What the...

anging... swinging... my dreams snapped me into reality! I first realized I couldn't touch the ground. *There was no ground*! My hands were above my head, clamped together. No - tied together! My eyes slowly adjusted to the dark room, enough to make out faint images and shapes. Sparse furnishings, a desk and a couple chairs. I turned my head upwards and saw my hands duct-taped together and tied to a pipe that ran across the ceiling. I was in some type of warehouse. I had spent enough of my childhood in them to know that. I closed my eyes to listen better. Silence, I couldn't hear anyone or anything. That was good, maybe I could get out of this mess before my abductor came back! I knew my way around warehouses, but I had to get free first!

My legs were tied also, but not as tight. I forced them as far apart as possible, hoping to slacken the bindings around them. There wasn't any furniture close enough in front of my legs to use as leverage and I couldn't see behind me. I swung my legs, hoping to hit an object in back of me. They struck a large mass. That was good but I couldn't very well climb backwards. My human body wouldn't be able to bend in that direction. At this moment I wished I had superhuman powers and could disintegrate the tape and ropes that bound me. I swung again behind me with as much force as I could muster. "Shlt Nu!!" came a familiar voice.

The sound of his voice both startled me and sent a wave of relief rippling through my body. "La Tige?"

"The one and only. You're awake," replied La Tige.

"Yeah... I was in your office and... I was looking for you." An image of Kacy hunched with the tear gas canister flashed through my mind. *Oh crap, where is she?* One wave of relief was all I was allowed as torrents of fear washed over me again. My eyes still adjusting to the dark searched for her form. I swung and twisted my body in every way possible. The duct tape bindings limited my movements.

"What are you looking for?" sounded La Tige's voice from behind me.

"Kacy, where is she? Have you seen her?"

"I think she is on the other end of this pipe. Looks like you found me. I've been here for days. Someone shot me with some type of dart from behind and left me here. They haven't been back." The chill in the air caught me and sent a ripple up my spine.

The realization smacking me in the face, "They haven't been back. We are bound and hung and left to die? Who the heck tied me here?"

"Great question, suppose I was passed out when he brought you in. Now that you're here we can work together to get out," was his logical cop response.

"Kacy!" I shouted, but got no response.

"You can't help her bound like a roasting pig so let's work on getting ourselves free." La Tige logic. He was right. I couldn't help her so long as I was stuck to the pipe.

"There is a wall in front of me. I couldn't reach it by myself but if you can swing again hard enough I think I can get my legs on it and climb up."

I swung with all my might several times until the pain in my wrists was overwhelmed with numbness. He was able to use the wall as leverage to get up to the pipe where he was able to stabilize himself and use his mouth to gnaw at the duct tape binding him.

My hearing and eyes had adjusted to the darkness and I heard a stir at the other end of the pipe. *Kacy?* I heard something else. "Shh... Stop for a minute. I think someone is outside the building. Listen it sounds like jingling keys."

"There is someone outside, I can hear their footsteps. I'm almost loose," he mumbled with a mouth full of tape.

The door opened, light beamed from behind a wall and a shadow walked in. I couldn't see a face against the darkness contrasting with the light but he was tall and thin and I could smell fast food, my keen dumpster diving senses told me it was Burger King.

"My friends, are you hungry?" boomed a familiar male voice.

I hadn't eaten fast food in a long time, not since my street urchin days, but at the moment it smelled good and my stomach ached for the nasty greasiness of fries and a burger. No way I'd eat anything he gave me though! He drugged me once with some kind of *Dexter* tranquilizer. Who knows what he'd stuck inside the food. Yes, I'd been watching a lot of TV since departing to my safe haven paradise in the Caribbean.

"I'm sorry, La Tige, that I have kept you here for so very long without a bite to eat but I had to catch your little friend. She is a tricky one and she brought me a cute little friend. You both need to disappear together, but first we'll talk. I wouldn't want you to die before you knew why." *How kind of him to put our well-being first.*

I knew the voice, it was a familiar one in my head as my mind replayed: *Celia will be here in two days; maybe she is worth giving a chance*. Alberto! He tricked me. He knew my instinct would be to run. I couldn't face her and he needed me away from Ashla so he could *take care* of me without her knowing. He actually had me believing that he was a victim. No, he's the psychopath. He killed all those men, *but was she part of it?* My mind still thinking her innocent; the story, the brother, all of it made up? Or was it just him? My mind was inclined to believe they were in it together.

I boldly asked, "Is she part of this, too?"

"You will get your turn, now is mine!" He shouted loud enough for the sound waves to bounce off the walls and echo, emphasizing *mine, mine, mine.*

He sauntered towards La Tige, who was still hanging from the pole. "You, it took me a while to figure out that it was you. You're not much to look at. I don't get why she has spent all these years pining over you? He sent me to find her and kill her. He couldn't do it. In the hospital I slipped in and out like a ghost with her tugging along. I drove her across state lines while she slept off the sedative I'd given her. I couldn't do it. I couldn't kill her. I left her sleeping on a motel bed in Nevada and faked her death. I collected my money and then killed him! The most relishing kill of my career! Until now, now I get both of you!" his voice calm and revealing.

Why was he referring to La Tige? Aallyah, the name I found In hls cabinet. Ashla is his wife? I remembered the day he gave me the key to his unsolved cases drawer. She was his unsolved case!

Alberto looked at me. "I told you the truth. You are her niece and your mother," his voice snarling, "will be in Puerto Rico tomorrow and she will be so upset to find that you have run away again," his voice now mocking me. "The best kills are the ones I do for free. Please ask me now what is it you want to know? Is she part of this? No, she is innocent. She really believes her husband is alive and trying to kill her. Now that is funny!" He chuckled. "She loves me and I believe I love her. That's why I couldn't kill her. I have to keep her at a distance. She can't know what I do! I help her hide and lead her to her next husband, whom I have already vetted. Once his money is mine, he dies," he said with no remorse in his voice. The entire story became clear and I punched myself mentally for thinking Ashla was a party to his demented ways.

This man was insane! He used her and thinks he loves her. *Is it written in my DNA to be attracted to trouble? To have sociopaths hidden in every corner?! Is this my life?* Raul's dark wavy hair and chiseled chest swam into my mind. To think I'd considered maybe he was the killer made guilt flood my body.

He sauntered away from us, cool as an autumn evening and headed towards Kacy. "Wake up, princess. I want your naive little friend over there," his hand motioned in my direction, "to see how close we've become."

"Not Kacy," I whispered to La Tige who took advantage of Alberto's departure across the room. "Hurry."

My mind had drifted from the pain in my hands and centered on my best friend. I had to stop the beast. He couldn't harm Kacy but I was duct-taped to a pipe. "Hey asshole," I had no idea where my mind was going but the nasty words flowed. "Creep face. You are the lowest form of roach I've ever met and Ashla deserves so much better than you!" I shouted. He stopped in his tracks and chuckled, then continued his beeline towards Kacy.

I could barely see his form and had no ideas. My mind raced for any idea to get us out of the jam. I'd been in plenty of messes, but none that included other innocent people, especially those I cared for. This was my worst nightmare.

"You bitch!" came from Alberto from the other end of the dark warehouse. *Go Kacy,* I thought. Then a *thunk* loud enough to jar my brain. He's hit her, that pig! I heard a scuffle.

"Kacy!" I shouted, unaware at first the voice emanated from me. His form moved closer to me, dragging Kacy. She struggled against his form as he dragged her towards us.

"Stop fighting you little wench!" he seethed.

"Let go of me asshole!" Kacy sneered as she kicked and struggled against his strength. *Thwack* as he kicked her in the face. Her head falling backwards against the blow. She became quiet and motionless. My heart ceased to beat for a second as I grasped that he knocked her unconscious - I hoped. If he killed her with that blow I would kill him in cold blood and without mercy!

"Stay put you little bitch," he wailed as he tossed her limp body to the side as if she was nothing more than a dead rat.

He turned towards us and I scooted next to La Tige. I was sure that La Tige was free, but so far he'd been silent except for the sound of his breathing. While Alberto was busy with La Tige I diverted my attention to my best friend lying still on the floor beside me. "Kacy," I whispered, hoping to hear her stir - nothing. Slowly I dragged my foot in her direction hoping to nudge her back, but I couldn't reach. *Damn my shortness!*

I diverted my attention towards La Tige and Alberto. He held the hamburger up to La Tige's nose and said, "You must be hungry. I've been rude, but here, eat." His voice was calm and detached. La Tige turned his head so the burger hit his cheek. Boy, was this guy a psychopath, battering Kacy unconscious one minute, then calmly offering La Tige food the next.

I couldn't see what happened next because it hurt too much to keep my head strained towards my back. The pain in my hands and wrists temporarily reminded me I was still tied to a pipe. This was no time for self-pity and pain. I pushed the burn and stinging out of my thoughts and concentrated on the scuffle emerging behind me, gargling, choking sounds and then a thud as Alberto hit floor. His face and body immobile to the side of me.

The next thing I knew, La Tige searched Alberto, his pockets inside his jacket and then he exclaimed, "Here it is!" A shiny, jingling object flashed in his hand. He ran-hobbled towards one of the chairs and dragged it closer to me, climbed on top of it and cut my ropes.

"Is he dead?" I asked, wishing for a 'yes, the bastard is gone'. Instead, I got in a stern voice, "Hold as still as you can while I cut these off you." I held still, my thoughts raging with questions and the thought of making sure Alberto was gone for good, but I didn't talk until he was done and gently allowed me to slip through his arms to the floor. My wrlsts were swollen and bleeding, but my hands were free! La Tige slashed the duct tape around my legs.

The first thing I did was kick Alberto's tall form several times with force in the head. "This is for Kacy," *thunk*, "for La Tige," *thunk*, "for me," *thunk*, "for Ashla," *thunk*.

In his most inflexible voice, with Kacy in his thick arms, La Tige barked, "Are you done? Now, let's go!"

"I have to make sure. Don't you watch movies? If you don't kill them when they're down they come back and kill you!" I said, frantic and hyped up on adrenaline.

He offered no response, instead rushed towards the area we saw the light beaming moments earlier - the door. Kacy in his arms. His limp more evident than usual with the extra weight of my best friend. I followed him through the darkness and we found the door. With painstaking care he lowered Kacy to the ground and fumbled with the lock, but it was locked from the inside. He jammed key after key into the lock, none turned offering us safety. "Damnit! Bastard must have another set of keys. You wait here!" he demanded.

I waited and knelt on the cold stone floor beside Kacy. I lifted my swollen, bloody hands above her face. Heat radiated from her nose caused from her shallow breaths, then I pressed my head against her chest and a steady but weak heartbeat told me she was alive but needed medical care. I wasn't going back in there - Kacy needed me.

My ears keener as the darkness didn't allow my eyes to see everything. I heard La Tige rifle through Alberto's person. Then I heard the jingle of keys and another commotion. *He wasn't dead yet?* I should have given him a few more *thunks* to the head. My curlosity and desire to survive were too keen so I dared to look, peeking my head around the corner. Shadow images danced in the darkness. La Tige, the larger form, held Alberto, the skinny form, squirming with his bare arms around Alberto's neck and then Alberto stopped. I backed myself into my former position on the floor beside Kacy like a scared child.

La Tige returned and rifled through the keys, trying them all until one worked. Finally, after being trapped inside that building for however long, I expected daylight but instead I got night. The bay breeze chilly against my skin, I shivered and wrapped my body around Kacy as best I could. I had to keep her warm. La Tige pulled out a phone. "He didn't take your phone?"

His warm blue eyes stared back at mine while he called 9-1-1. Then his body collapsed. I rushed to him just in time to pad his fall as we both hit the ground. I managed to slip his bulk off my chest. There was no point to attempt and pull him closer to Kacy, so I opted to pull her closer, wrapping my small frame around them and cried as all the emotions I'd felt over the past forty-eight hours or so coursed through my body.

In a daze, lights from police cruisers and ambulances flashed around me. Cops and paramedics swarmed to my side, lifting me off my loved ones' cold but still breathing bodies.

"Miss, can you hear me?" voiced a paramedic, as he checked my eyes and pulse. "She's in shock," he said as they attempted to put me on a stretcher. I had to be stronger than that. I was stronger than that. I'd faced my fears, lost loved ones, and yet survived. Out of shear willpower life flashed back to the present and I jumped to my feet, rushing to the open ambulance as the other sped away, its lights flashing against the darkness of the night and siren wailing for everyone else to get out of the way.

Return to the Bay
Baby Girl VI

Triage

I jumped into the back of the ambulance just as they were closing the doors. A sharp pain originating from my mid section radiated throughout my body, shortening my breaths. I clutched my stomach, ignoring the fire inside me. A male paramedic caught my hand and helped me up. I looked into his hard brown eyes. They softened as he gently twisted my arm and gawked at my purple bloodied wrists. "You can stay, but keep to the side. Your friend is in bad shape." Wrapping my small hand around La Tige's chunky one, I closed my grip as tight as possible. The stinging in my wrists minimal.

"Thank you," I whispered.

I stayed out of the way but didn't let go of La Tige's hand. The pain in my side receded as the ambulance sped through the city and my mind raced. I couldn't focus on any one thought except *Are they going to be OK*? They had to be. I loved them both - my surrogate family.

"How do you feel?" asked a female paramedic, interrupting my thoughts. Her long blonde hair pulled back into a tight pony tail.

"Confused, scared."

She squatted in front of me. Pointing to her partner she said, "He's got your friend. I'm going to take care of you." Her voice calm.

I gazed at La Tige's face. HIs eyes closed as if in a deep sleep and a mask over his nose for oxygen I assumed. She felt for my pulse, checked my blood pressure and looked into my eyes. "Everything checks out, but your blood pressure is a little high. You need to calm down."

"I'm trying," I said, the words choking in my throat.

She held out my arms. "This doesn't look good, but it will heal. I noticed you wincing when you hopped on board. Are you sore anywhere else?"

I nodded my head, "My mid section."

She brought her hand to my mid section. "I'm going to touch your stomach and along your sides. You tell me where it hurts," She gently pressed her fingers against me. The entire area was tender but not agonizing. Then she pushed against my left ribcage and fire burst through my side.

"There," I squeaked.

She continued pressing her fingers in various areas. "He's going to be OK," she reassured, then described what her partner was doing with La Tige. Most of it went in one ear and out the other. I know she was talking to me just to calm me down.

She nodded, "You may have bruised or broken ribs. You'll need to be admitted to the hospital as well."

I shook my head. "What about Kacy?" I asked.

"The young lady? We can radio the other ambulance and find out." As she said that the ambulance pulled into the hospital ER loop. "Here we are. You'll find out soon. There's a waiting room inside the double doors, wait there."

I nodded.

They rolled La Tige out of the back of the ambulance. His large frame so fragile on the stretcher as they raced him through the hospital. Kacy was already inside, somewhere. I saw the waiting room and, understanding there was nothing more I could do for the moment, I took a seat. I stayed put for maybe five minutes before I started pacing, ignoring the throbbing in my side. Taking deep breaths I tried to control the convulsions of fear riding through my body. But inhaling large breaths hurt too much, so I settled for shallow ones.

"Cleo," called a male voice.

I turned and met eyes with Javier, Kacy's sexy boyfriend. I ran to him and folded my arms around him, taking care not to make sudden movements. My body shook and tears flowed over my cheeks and onto his shirt.

He rubbed my back. "He's a tough guy, honey. It'll take a lot more than that to take him down. Why don't we sit?" He guided me away from the ER waiting room and into a far quieter one. We sat on the couch.

"Would you like a soda or coffee?"

"No, I don't think I can hold anything down right now," I said through sobs.

He clucked his tongue. "How do you feel?"

"My ribs are-"

"Miss," called a nurse, wearing purple scrubs and white hospital-style shoes. Her gray hair wrapped in a bun with wiry bangs.

"Yes," I stood.

She took a step back and grabbed the handles of a wheel chair, "Are you with Mr. La Tige?"

"Yes. Do they know something already?" I asked, thinking it was far too soon for any answers.

"No, not yet. I was told you need medical assistance."

I remembered the female paramedic's words and cringing with each breath walked towards her as she said, "Come with me. I have orders to get you into triage."

All's Well That Ends Well

La Tige had been deprived of food and water for days. An intravenous tube was attached to his arm feeding him fluids, sustaining his life. A monitor beeped every few seconds letting us know his heart was still pumping. He had saved me and Kacy from Alberto. Not only a surrogate father, but a brave one that risked everything and found the inner strength to carry Kacy out of the warehouse. His body had been working off adrenaline until safety found us, then he collapsed like a huge grizzly bear. I softened his fall, which inadvertently bruised my ribs. My injuries were minor and my concern was La Tige. The bandages around my wrists covered the burns and scrapes from the ropes used to tie us up. The scars would forever be a reminder.

Kacy had suffered a slight concussion and had a huge knot on the back of her head but was fully awake, keeping vigil with me next to La Tige. I refused to leave his side and she refused to leave mine. At first the staff grumbled at her for not staying in her room. After they saw how stubborn she was they gave up, accepting they could still keep an eye on her from La Tige's room. She hated all their poking and prodding. Being coddled wasn't her thing.

The trouble had started out innocently. La Tige's job for me was to watch Ashla. We thought her a Black Widow. She had a string of dead, wealthy husbands, and various identities. My job was to watch her from afar, but I couldn't do that. I tried, but got strung along into Alberto's web of deceit. My weakness had been his mention of my bio-mom and the similarities I'd seen between Ashla and myself. Instead of a Black Widow, I began to think of her as an innocent victim of a psychopath. And she was. We were both blinded to Alberto being the psychopath.

He'd been hired to kill her but couldn't bring himself to do it, instead he used her fear to manipulate situations and had her believing her crazy husband was stalking her and killing off her husbands. In reality, Alberto had killed her husbands, all of them, except one. She believed Alberto to be her lover, tried and true. He didn't love her. He was obsessed and enjoyed the control he had over her, yanking her strings. She was still in Puerto Rico and had no idea anything had transpired. La Tige had used Alberto's phone to call 911 and they kept it as evidence. I wanted the phone to call her.

I told the story to the police officer in my statement but they were still confused. "How again does La Tige fall into this?" questioned a young cop with curly ginger hair and brown eyes.

I twisted at the tape around my left wrist and drew in a deep breath. For the fourth time today I recalled all the dirty details of mine and La Tige's connection. "The husband he hadn't killed was La Tige which is where I came in. Her first husband had been abusive and her father, in order to protect her, had sent her to the U.S. - New York - to live with her half-sister, my bio-mom, whom she'd never met. My bio-mom had... was a twin but her twin had died at birth so Ashla's father gave her my bio-mom's dead sister's name. Eventually she made it to California. I don't know the details, but she met La Tige and they got married. Soon she got pregnant but lost the baby at birth." I was piecing together all my gathered knowledge as best I could.

"Alberto comes into the picture here and kidnaps her from the hospital. I don't know how the hospital didn't catch him, but he's sly. According to Alberto he was supposed to kill her but couldn't because he "loves" her. Instead, he tricked her into thinking that her abusive husband was hunting her down. He's already killed him. Did I say that yet? I think... I forgot."

He looked at me pensively and I could hear his brain rattling as it tried to make sense of what I was telling him. "Alberto killed all her husbands but La Tige. How does she come in?" he asked, shifting his gaze in Kacy's direction.

She rolled her eyes, as tired of replaying the story as I was. "I live here. When Cleo called me and said

La Tige was missing I picked her up at the airport and we went by his office to look for clues that would tell us where he was. We heard a sound, stopped in our tracks and that's it. He shot some type of tranquilizing darts into our necks and we blacked out, waking up in the warehouse. I'm tired of reliving all this. Do you have Alberto? Is he dead?"

He sucked in his breath laboriously, then let it out slow and controlled. "Nobody was inside the warehouse. We searched it and are still searching the surrounding area. This isn't to say we don't believe you. Something happened that traumatized both of you, and this man here," he pointed towards La Tige, "has been through hell. We are trying to piece together what happened. When we know more, so will you." Then he stood and held out a business card, "Here is my card. My number at the precinct is on it." He flipped it over and scribbled something on the back. "That's my cell phone. Don't hesitate to call." Then he was gone.

I thought of Ashla. She needed to know the story. She was an innocent victim…

Bright Eyed and Frumpy Tailed

I felt a warm, big hand clutch mine and my eyes fluttered open to La Tige's looking at me filled with love. I jumped off the small sofa I positioned beside his bed and rushed him with a huge hug, forgetting my ribs were still a bit sore. "You're awake!" I shouted, ignoring the sting festering my side.

"Quiet. You'll alert the staff," he muttered. His usual charming self.

Kacy stirred and wiped her hands across her eyes as she stretched her body across the couch she'd fallen asleep on. She peered at me through one eye as her hand lingered above the other then with a blast of wakefulness, shouted, "You're awake!" she rushed his other side, thanking him for saving our lives.

He lay in bed as we reached around him, each pecking a cheek.

"Careful," he muttered as he lifted his arms and folded one around each of us. The hug lasted only a moment as his arms were still weak.

I plopped onto the sofa. "We've been here beside your bed for forty-nine hours," I pronounced as I eyed the clock.

Kacy sank onto the couch and blurted out, "I've been thinking a lot about your story," she looked at me curiously, "it doesn't add up. How did Alberto get here from Puerto Rico and kidnap La Tige without you noticing his absence? It's not like the island is as close as Alcatraz. I mean it took you two flights and several hours. And where is his body? I know I was unconscious during the rescue but I've heard you play through the story over and over. He had to be dead or at least in a very bad way. How could he just disappear?"

She was right. I had never lost sight of Ashla and Alberto for more than a few hours. Certainly not enough time for him to get to San Francisco, kidnap La Tige and then get back. *Why hadn't I thought of that?* "Because he has an accomplice?"

"I taught you well," chuckled La Tige. He appeared to be getting a kick out of watching me and Kacy take on his detective role.

I paced the room for a few minutes but had no idea who could be helping him unless... It wasn't Ashla, and at this point I believed Raul to be in the clear. *Oh my crackers!* I hadn't had a chance to tell Kacy about him. It would have to wait. There were more important things right now.

The nurse strolled in. "Time to check on the patient," she nodded her head in approval. "Mr. La Tige, you're awake. Welcome back. I'll get the doctor." She strolled back out the door.

"I gotta go. I need to go back to your office," I roared. The wheels were spinning in my head.

"I'm going with you!" shouted Kacy.

The doctor gallivanted in as if he owned the place. I gave La Tige a peck on the cheek and left him with the doc. He was in good hands.

"You better be back up!" La Tige hollered after us. In his weakened state he wasn't as loud as usual.

Kacy hauled butt after me and we rushed to the elevator. The adrenaline pumping fast in my veins. We were on to something, but what I had no idea. Kacy jumped In front of me and held up her hand against my chest. "We're rushing in without a plan, a cell phone, or back up. You heard La Tige, and if there's an accomplice out there I don't want to end up dead. He... or she, might not be as clumsy as Alberto."

She was right. I looked around. A nurses' station was just to my right. Kacy caught on to my thoughts and walked up to the nurses' station with me in tow this time. "Excuse me," she cut in.

The nurse behind the desk was a young woman no older than ourselves with gentle brown eyes and a warm smile. "Can I help you?"

"Do you have a phone we can use?"

She opened her mouth, most likely to say no, then shut it. She punched out her lips, drew them back in and looked around. "Be quick," she said and handed us the hospital phone.

"I got this," Kacy stated as she dialed a number. "We need your help..." She told the mystery person where we were and said, "We'll be waiting."

I looked at her expectantly, widened my eyes, and drew my still sore hands out in front of me in a *so what* gesture.

"That was Big Billy. He's going to pick us up," she stated, shrugging her shoulders in response to my *so what* gesture.

www.ingramcontent.com/pod-product-compliance
Lightning Source LLC
Chambersburg PA
CBHW050537190726
48284CB00003B/1106